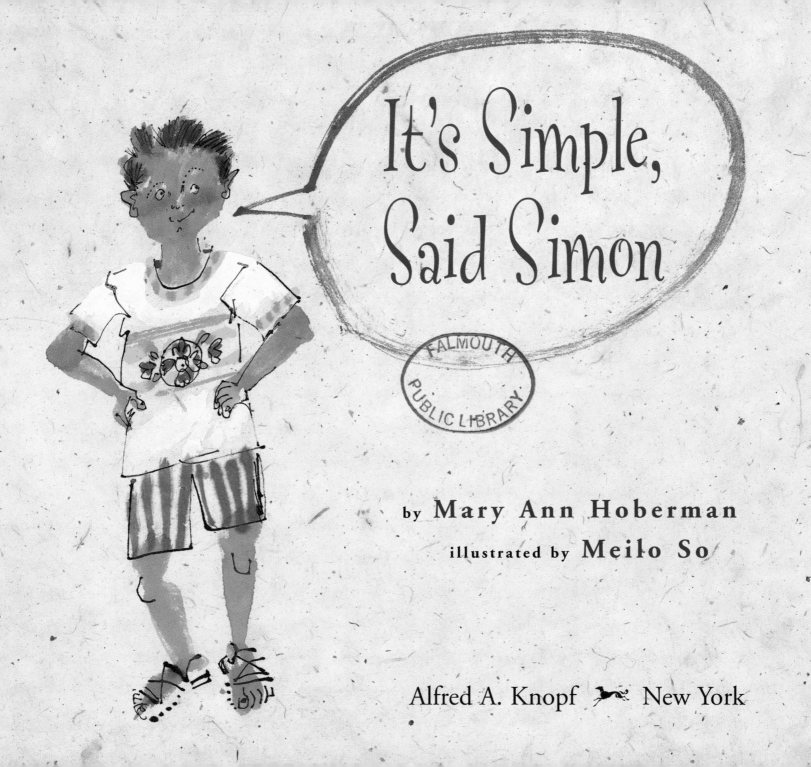

It's Simple, Said Simon

by **Mary Ann Hoberman**

illustrated by **Meilo So**

Alfred A. Knopf 🐎 New York

To Theo Moszynski, with much love—M.A.H.

To Joe and Brightness—M.S.

One day, Simon met a dog.

"I bet you can't growl," growled the dog.

Simon growled a low growl.

"Very good," said the dog.

"It's simple," said Simon.

Next, Simon met a cat.

"I bet you can't stretch," purred the cat.

Simon stretched a small stretch.

"Very good," said the cat.

"It's simple," said Simon.

Farther on, Simon met a horse.

"I bet you can't jump," neighed the horse.

Simon jumped a short jump.

"Very good," said the horse.
"It's simple," said Simon.

Then Simon met a tiger.

"I bet you can't growl," growled the tiger.

Simon growled a low growl.

"That's not loud enough," growled the tiger.

Simon growled **a louder growl.**

"Still not loud enough," growled the tiger.

Simon growled a really loud growl.

"Very good," said the tiger.

"It's simple," said Simon.

"I bet you can't stretch," said the tiger.

Simon stretched a small stretch.
"That's not long enough," said the tiger.

Simon stretched a longer stretch.

"Still not long enough," said the tiger.

Simon stretched a really long stretch.

"Very good," said the tiger.
"It's simple," said Simon.
"I bet you can't jump," said the tiger.

Simon jumped a short jump.

"That's not high enough," said the tiger.

a higher jump.

Simon jumped

"Still not high enough," said the tiger.

a really high jump.

Simon jumped

"Very good," said the tiger.

"It's simple," said Simon.

"I bet you can't jump up on my back," said the tiger.

Simon jumped up on the tiger's back.

"Now I've got you," said the tiger,
and off he trotted into the jungle.

It began to get dark.

"Could you please take me home now?" said
Simon. "It's almost suppertime, and I'm hungry."
"I am, too," said the tiger.

"I'm having an egg for my supper," said Simon.
"I'm having a boy for mine," said the tiger.

"I'm thirsty," said Simon.

"I am, too," said the tiger, and he ambled down to the river.

"I can't reach the water," said Simon.
The tiger waded out a little.

"I still can't reach it," said Simon.
The tiger waded out a little farther.

"I still can't quite reach it," said Simon.

The tiger waded out as far as he could.
Simon leaped off his back and began to swim.

"Help!" yelled the tiger.
"I can't swim!"

"It's simple," said Simon.

And he swam down the river and got home
just in time for supper.

This is a Borzoi Book Published by Alfred A. Knopf

Text copyright © 2001 by Mary Ann Hoberman
Illustrations copyright © 2001 by Meilo So
All rights reserved under International and Pan-American Copyright Conventions. Published in the
United States of America by Alfred A. Knopf , a division of Random House, Inc., New York,
and simultaneously in Canada by Random House of Canada Limited, Toronto.
Distributed by Random House, Inc., New York.

www.randomhouse.com/kids

Library of Congress Cataloging-in-Publication Data

Hoberman, Mary Ann.
"It's simple," said Simon / by Mary Ann Hoberman ; illustrated by Meilo So.—1st ed.
p.   cm.
Summary: After successfully meeting the challenges posed by a dog, cat, and horse, Simon meets a tiger
that is much harder to satisfy and that he must outwit before he becomes the tiger's dinner.
ISBN 0-375-81201-6 (trade) — ISBN 0-375-91201-0 (lib. bdg.)
[1. Tigers—Fiction. 2. Humorous stories.] I. So, Meilo, ill. II. Title.

PZ7.H6525 It 2001
[E]—dc21
00-042831

Printed in the United States of America

March, 2001

First Edition

10   9   8   7   6   5   4   3   2   1